Black Beauty
and the Thunderstorm

story by **SUSAN HILL**
illustrated by **BILL FARNSWORTH**

inspired by **ANNA SEWELL**'s *Black Beauty*

SQUARE
FISH

Macmillan Children's Publishing Group
New York

CHAPTER ONE
My Own True Name

I have had many names.

But the name I knew first,

the one that is my own true name,

is Black Beauty.

When I was young,
I lived in a green meadow
and ran free with my mother
and my friends.

Then I was sold.

I had a lot of bad luck

and worse owners.

Finally, a cabdriver named Jerry

became my new master.

Jerry's family ran out to greet us
when we got to the big city.
Everyone spoke at once.
"Let's call him Jack!"
said a girl named Dolly.

"He's a beauty,"
said Jerry's wife.
"Can I ride him?" asked Dolly.
Jerry laughed and patted my neck.

"You are not a city horse,"
Jerry said to me.
"And driving a cab is hard work.
But I can see by your manner
that you're a good horse.
I hope we will get along."

Chapter Two
Oats and Hay and Braids

That night,

I ate a good meal of oats and hay.

Then Dolly came out to the stable

to visit me.

She began to brush my sides.

"How does that feel, Jack?" she asked.

I couldn't tell her how good it felt.

I couldn't say,

"Thank you, friend."

I put my nose into her hand instead.

15

Then she worked my mane

and tail into braids

as dark and gleaming as her own.

"You're as gentle as my kitten,

and just as pretty,"

she said when she was done.

"Pretty Jack."

I prefer "handsome,"

but I was glad she liked

the look of me.

CHAPTER THREE
City Streets

The work was hard.

I was not used to the noise

or the crowds.

There were streets crossing each other

for mile upon mile, all of them clogged

with cabs and carriages,

trucks and wagons.

I watched my step

and let Jerry guide me.

Suddenly, a horse and cart
raced through a busy crossing
in such a hurry
that we nearly collided.

I stopped sharply
and raised my front legs
to get out of the way.
The horse and cart
crashed into a fruit stall
and came to a stop.

A grim-looking man
in a coat with shiny buttons
swaggered across the street.
"You, cabbie!" he shouted to Jerry.
"Mind your horse!"
 "My horse had the good sense to stop
before I even saw that reckless cart,"
said Jerry calmly.

The man with shiny buttons frowned.

"Well, mind the beast, I say,

or he'll hurt someone!"

"Click, click, Jack," said Jerry.

We drove on.

CHAPTER FOUR
A Storm in the Night

One terrible night,

Dolly came to see me.

Thunder grumbled like

an angry master.

Lightning cracked like a whip.

"I don't like storms," she said.

Suddenly, Dolly's cat ran out

of the stable yard.

"Stop!" shouted Dolly.

Then she went after him—
out into the terrible night!
I reared and whinnied,
but nobody came.

I had to go after her myself.

I rammed the gate till it broke,

cutting my leg.

Then I ran out into the storm.

I looked everywhere for Dolly.

The night was so dark,

I could hardly see.

Sheets of rain ran off my sides,

and I was freezing cold.

My leg bled.

Where could she be?

I went toward the river.

Lightning cracked,

and suddenly,

the man with shiny buttons

jumped in front of me.

He startled me, so I reared up!

He tried to grab my mane.

My hooves came crashing down.

The man fell to the ground,

and then it was dark again.

The night went quiet,

and I could hear the river rushing.

I heard a whimper.

I hurried toward the sound,

and in the next flash of light,

I saw two sopping braids.

I found Dolly!

She had fallen into the river.
She was struggling in the icy water
and trying to hold onto her cat.
She could not fight the current
much longer.
I heard her call my name,
but her voice was weak.
The river was sweeping her away!

I ran along the bank
till I saw her clinging to a rock.
Our eyes met,
but she was too afraid to move.
"I can't!" she cried.
I had to get her out
before it was too late!

35

Carefully, I stepped down
the muddy bank.
I turned my tail to her and
tossed my head up and down.
Dolly gripped my tail
with one hand.

In her other hand,
she held her cat.
I pulled her out of the river
and up the bank.

A small voice inside of me said,

"Run free, now! Run to the meadow!"

But I did not.

I led Dolly home.

Chapter Five

Home

The next day,

the man with shiny buttons came.

His cheek was scratched

and his arm was bound in a sling,

but he was not badly hurt.

He was angry.

"Your horse almost killed me

last night!" he said.

"He's as wild as the storm!"

Jerry frowned.

"This horse went out into the storm and brought my little girl back. He saved her life."

"If you can't control the beast,

you must get rid of him,"

said the man with shiny buttons.

Jerry shook his head firmly,

the way a horse will shake his head

to refuse a painful bit.

"No, I will not get rid of him,"

Jerry said in a voice both soft and strong.

The man with shiny buttons

stormed off.

And I got an extra pail of oats.

This city stable is not a green meadow,
and I do not run free.

Pretty Jack is not

my own true name.

But this is my family.

I am loved here,

and I am home.

Dear Parents and Teachers,

In an easy-reader format, **My Readers** introduce classic stories to children who are learning to read. Although favorite characters and time-tested tales are the basis for **My Readers**, the books tell completely new stories and are freshly and beautifully illustrated.

My Readers are available in three levels:

1 **Level One** is for the emergent reader and features repetitive language and word clues in the illustrations.

2 **Level Two** is for more advanced readers who still need support saying and understanding some words. Stories are longer with word clues in the illustrations.

3 **Level Three** is for independent, fluent readers who enjoy working out occasional unfamiliar words. The stories are longer and divided into chapters.

Encourage children to select books based on interests, not reading levels. Read aloud with children, showing them how to use the illustrations for clues. With adult guidance and rereading, children will eventually read the desired book on their own.

Here are some ways you might want to use this book with children:

- Talk about the title and the cover illustrations. Encourage the child to use these to predict what the story is about.
- Discuss the interior illustrations and try to piece together a story based on the pictures. Does the child want to change or adjust his first prediction?
- After children reread a story, suggest they retell or act out a favorite part.

My Readers will not only help children become readers, they will serve as an introduction to some of the finest classic children's books available today.

—LAURA ROBB
Educator and Reading Consultant

For Debbie
—B. F.

SQUARE
FISH

An Imprint of Macmillan Children's Publishing Group

Library of Congress Cataloging-in-Publication Data Available

ISBN 978-0-312-64705-6 (hardcover)
1 3 5 7 9 10 8 6 4 2

ISBN 978-0-312-64721-6 (paperback)
3 5 7 9 10 8 6 4

Book design by Patrick Collins/Véronique Lefèvre Sweet

Square Fish logo designed by Filomena Tuosto

First Edition: 2011

myreadersonline.com
mackids.com

This is a Level 3 book

LEXILE: 520L